小龍嗡嗡嗡

Lucy Kincaid 著

Eric Kincaid 繪

陳韋倩 譯

三民書局

The Little Dragon   ISBN 1 85854 777 6

Written by Lucy Kincaid and illustrated by Eric Kincaid

First published in 1998

Under the title The Little Dragon

by Brimax Books Limited

4/5 Studlands Park Ind. Estate,

Newmarket, Suffolk, CB8 7AU

小龍和兔子

Dragon and the Rabbits

One day the baby rabbits come to see Little Dragon.
"We want to **learn** to hum," they say.
Little Dragon **shakes** his head.
"You must go home to your mother," he says. "She will **worry** if she cannot **find** you."
The baby rabbits **hop** away into the wood.

learn [lɜn]
働 學習

shake [ʃek]
働 搖

worry [ˋwɜɪ]
働 擔心

find [faɪnd]
働 找到，發現

hop [hɑp]
働 跳

有一天，兔寶寶們來拜訪小龍。
「我們想學嗡嗡叫。」他們說。
小龍搖搖頭。
「你們得回家找媽媽呀！」他說。
「如果她沒看到你們的話，會很擔心的喲！」
兔寶寶們蹦蹦跳跳地走進了樹林裡頭。

Little Dragon is humming again.
The bees are humming too.
Along comes Mother Rabbit.
"Where are my babies?" asks
Mother Rabbit.
"I told them to go home to you,"
says Little Dragon.

小龍又嗡嗡嗡地哼著。
蜜蜂們也跟著嗡嗡嗡。
兔媽媽往這邊來了。
「我的小寶寶哪兒去了呢？」兔媽
媽問。
「我要他們回家找妳啊！」小龍說。

Mother Rabbit **calls** her babies.
They do not come.
Mother Rabbit begins to cry.
"I have **lost** my babies," she says.
"Do not cry," says Little Dragon.
"We will find your babies for you,"
say the bees.

兔媽媽呼喚她的小寶寶。
他們沒有來。
兔媽媽哭了起來。
「我把我的小寶寶弄丟了。」她說。
「不要哭！」小龍說。
「我們會幫妳找到妳的小寶寶。」
蜜蜂們說。

Little Dragon and Mother Rabbit **look for** the baby rabbits. The bees help too.

The baby rabbits have gone. Nobody can find them.

"They must be hiding," says Little Dragon.

小龍和兔媽媽在尋找兔寶寶。蜜蜂們也來幫忙。

兔寶寶不見了。沒有人找得到他們。

「他們一定是躲起來了。」小龍說。

Then Little Dragon stops.
He **stands still**.
"Listen!" he says. "I can hear something."
"So can I," says Mother Rabbit.
"So can we," say the bees.

然後小龍停了下來，站住不動。
「你們聽！」他說。「我聽到了什麼哦！」
「我也是。」兔媽媽說。
「我們也是。」蜜蜂們說。

Little Dragon **peeps** over the **bush**. Mother Rabbit and the bees look too. They see the baby rabbits sitting on the **grass**.

"What are they doing?" ask the bees.

The baby rabbits are trying to hum. They are trying very **hard**. But they cannot do it.

peep [pip]
動 偷看

bush [buʃ]
名 灌木叢

grass [græs]
名 草地

hard [hɑrd]
副 努力地

小龍從灌木叢中探頭出來張望。兔媽媽和蜜蜂們也跟著張望。他們看見兔寶寶們正坐在草地上。「他們在做什麼啊？」蜜蜂們問。兔寶寶們正試著嗡嗡叫呢！他們好努力地試了又試，可是還是做不到！

"Hello!" says Little Dragon. "What are you trying to do?"
The baby rabbits see Little Dragon.
They hop away and hide.
"Come out of there," says Little Dragon.

「哈囉！」小龍說。「你們在做什麼啊？」
兔寶寶們看見小龍，便一蹦一跳地跑開，躲了起來。
「出來啊！」小龍說。

The baby rabbits will not come
out. They do not see Mother Rabbit.
"Come out of there **at once**!" says
Mother Rabbit.
"Yes, Mother," say the baby
rabbits.

at once
立刻，馬上

兔ㄊㄨˋ寶ㄅㄠˇ寶ㄅㄠˇ們ㄇㄣˊ可ㄎㄜˇ不ㄅㄨˋ想ㄒㄧㄤˇ出ㄔㄨ來ㄌㄞˊ呢ㄋㄜ！他ㄊㄚ們ㄇㄣˊ並ㄅㄧㄥˋ
沒ㄇㄟˊ有ㄧㄡˇ看ㄎㄢˋ見ㄐㄧㄢˋ兔ㄊㄨˋ媽ㄇㄚ媽ㄇㄚ。
「馬ㄇㄚˇ上ㄕㄤˋ給ㄍㄟˇ我ㄨㄛˇ出ㄔㄨ來ㄌㄞˊ！」兔ㄊㄨˋ媽ㄇㄚ媽ㄇㄚ說ㄕㄨㄛ。
「是ㄕˋ的ㄉㄜ，媽ㄇㄚ媽ㄇㄚ。」兔ㄊㄨˋ寶ㄅㄠˇ寶ㄅㄠˇ們ㄇㄣˊ說ㄕㄨㄛ。

"Come with me," says Mother Rabbit. "We're going home at once."
The baby rabbits look very sad.
"What were they trying to do?" ask the bees.
"They were trying to hum, like us," says Little Dragon.

「跟我走。」兔媽媽說。「我們馬上就回家。」
兔寶寶們看起來好難過的樣子！
「他們剛剛在做什麼啊？」蜜蜂們問。
「他們想和我們一樣地嗡嗡嗡呢！」小龍說。

"We can **show** them how to hum," say the bees.

"Yes," says Little Dragon.

So they **follow** Mother Rabbit.

It takes a long time to show a rabbit how to hum. Little Dragon tries very hard. So do the bees.

At last the baby rabbits can do it.

show [ʃo]
動 教

follow [`falo]
動 跟隨

at last
終於，最後

「我們可以教他們怎麼嗡嗡叫啊！」蜜蜂說。
「對呀！」小龍說。
所以他們就跟著兔媽媽。
教兔子嗡嗡叫可得花不少時間，
小龍非常賣力地試了試。蜜蜂們也是。
兔寶寶們終於學會了。

Little Dragon is humming.
The bees are humming.
The rabbits are humming.
"I didn't know rabbits could hum,"
says **Owl**.
"My babies are the only rabbits that
can," says Mother Rabbit.

owl [aʊl]
名 貓頭鷹

小龍嗡嗡嗡。
蜜蜂們嗡嗡嗡。
兔子們嗡嗡嗡。
「我可不知道兔子會嗡嗡嗡呢！」
貓頭鷹說。
「我的寶寶是唯一一會嗡嗡嗡的兔子喲！」兔媽媽說。

兒童文學叢書

小詩

有一種，在不遠不近的
林子裡邊，說：
「七就七，九歸九？」
（早安，吃飽了沒？）
我知道，牠們就是白頭翁。

（摘自《家是我放心的地方》
林煥彰／詩，施政廷／畫）

系列

在六點五點之間，
早起的鳥兒，
有很多種，不同的叫聲；